The Man Who Wore A Red Cape

By David Evans

Table of Contents

Chapter 1 2

Chapter 2 13

Chapter 3 23

Chapter 4 32

Chapter 5 44

Chapter 6 54

Chapter One: An Introduction to the family

Mr. Ruffalo, was so obsessed with the comics and the action hero's that he wanted to be like superman, who wears a red cape. He had some old capes down in the basement but his favorite cape was the red one. It wasn't as long as he wanted it to be, so he made it longer.

He found more material and hemmed it together to the length that he preferred. He has a young son and daughter, his sons name is Huey and his daughters name is Alexis. His son's turning seven years old this year and his daughter is eight years old and loves to play around in the yard and act like a tom boy.

While his son likes to pick up sticks and throw them at the house, He tries to teach them good lessons on how to behave, when he has the time. One time He was trying to teach his son, how to play baseball and he accidentally threw the baseball through the bedroom window.

The window shattered into hundreds of pieces which took him several minutes to clean up the glass. That same day Huey was walking in the backyard and tripped over something and tore up his knee. He cried, then calmed down once his dad held his hand.

Look, you can't be a cry baby, you need to get tough, you're a boy not a girl and I wish that you would play some football in school. You would make a good quarter back on a football team. I don't like to get run into by other players, and it makes my body hurt. You will learn how to take the harsh impacts and you will grow a strong body.

"Why are you so obsessed with football?"

"I just like it."

You watch football games every night and don't focus on me enough. I'm sorry that I have ignored you these past few days, I have to spend some time with your sister too. Dad she ripped up my last power rangers coloring book and broke one of my crayons.

It'll be okay, she tends to do that sometimes, but I love my power ranger coloring books and she just rips them up like they mean nothing to her. I have heard enough, why don't you go back to your room and take out your new dinosaur coloring book that I got you last year.

"Dad could you please color with me?"

"Yes," I will color with you.

"Where's mom?"

"She's probably at work right now, because it's going on eleven fifteen."

"Why does mom have to work?"

"To earn money."

"Do you have a lot of money

"No"

To survive in this world you need money and you're too young to understand money and how it works. You will learn about money soon enough, you know dad I wish I was old like you.

"What you are telling me that I'm old?"

"Yes," dad you are old but not as old as grandpop.

"Why would you say something so silly."

"Where's my sister at?"

"She's running around the living room."

Dad please stay in my room a minute or two longer with me. I will spend an hour in your room with you coloring, why don't you lay on the floor with me and color.

I will help you color, but I'm not going to lay on my stomach and color like you. You used to be more fun just a few years ago, I know but I'm going through what you call a mid-life crisis and I need a shrink to talk to.

"What's a shrink?"

"It's someone that helps you to get your thoughts back together."

You never told me about that

"How often do you have to go to a shrink?"

"I go to a shrink every Thursday and that's why your mom has to cook for you two on a Thursday night."

"How long do you have to be at the shrink for?"

"It all depends on me."

Sometimes when I feel really bad about myself I will stay and talk to the shrink for two hours. I hope that you no longer get sad, thanks, but I'm bound to get sad again soon. Don't be so negative, maybe things will change for you in your life. Just having you and my daughter and my wife around makes me happy. You know mom is much younger then you are, I realize that. She's just four years younger than me, and it's no big deal.

"Why do you color so slowly?"

"So that I don't mess up the picture."

You know, I used to love when you would run around the house wearing that silly long red cape, it would make me and my sister laugh.

"Can we have the spicy cheese nachos?"

"Yes, I don't know how you like the hot stuff, but your mom likes hot stuff too"

Don't worry were going to have the spicy nachos for dinner tonight oh boy dad I can't wait.

"Can I have a cookie for dessert?"

"No," you have had enough cookies.

I saw you raid the cookie jar more than once yesterday. Besides that, the sugar in those cookies isn't good for you. I didn't know that, just remember father knows best.

"Is mom going to make more cookies?"

"If she has time I'm sure that she will."

You're going to have to ask her very nicely and she will make you a few dozen chocolate chip cookies.

"Why can't we just buy the cookies from the local grocery store?"

"First of all you know that your mom likes to bake cookies, and the cookies from the grocery store have more sugar in them then the cookies that your mom makes."

Thank you for the long explanation, I can color a lot quicker than you can, I don't want to rush while I'm coloring.

"Why can't you be like every other kid and not be so geeky?"

"It's how I am and you can't change me."

I love you dad and always will, when I'm an old man I want to be just like you. Awe, I love when you tell me that. It's true.

"How's Rascal doing?"

"I don't know where he is right now."

I love how Rascal runs around the house, he always puts on a smile on my face no matter how sad I feel.

"What kind of dog is Rascal?"

"He's a French bull dog"

We got him when you were five years old. We bought him at the local pet smart, he was a very expensive dog and I don't want to buy another dog once he passes away.

"How long will he live for?"

"That all depends on him."

"Do you ever get night mares about Rascal passing away?"

"No," and you have asked me too many questions.

"Where do all these questions come from?"

I just get curious and want to ask more questions, that's a good answer. I'm getting hungry for a cookie.

"Can I have one?"

"No," not yet you will have to wait until you are done with lunch.

"What am I going to have for lunch?"

"I'm going to make you a cheese burger in the microwave and I will make you fries to go along with it."

That sounds good, but I prefer my cheeseburger to be cooked in the oven.

"Must you always make me do a lot of extra work?"

"No," dad, I just think the cheeseburgers taste better when cooked in the oven.

We never have much time, because it goes by so fast. I know but I'm tired of you making all of my food in the microwave. I want to go and take a walk around the block to burn off some energy.

Yes, we can do that, but I don't know if Alexis would like to do that. She's a princess and probably won't want to run around like I do. Don't talk about your sister like that.

Rascal came running into the room with his tongue hanging out and slobber going all over the carpet. Rascal you slobber too much, let's play if you're going to play with Rascal you better be careful.

"Why must I be careful?"

"I don't like it when you cuddle up so close to his face."

I'm afraid that Rascal might end up biting you. You have a good looking face son and I don't want it to get all bit up and ruined. I don't want to have to take you to the hospital, please get away from his face. I will get away from his face.

"How's that?"

"That's better, now stand up son and run around with Rascal."

He just ran away from me and ran towards the kitchen. You're going to have to watch that rascal doesn't go to the bathroom on the nice Brazilian rug in the kitchen.

I thought that you taught Rascal better than that. No, he hasn't had much training, because your mother and I don't have much time to spend with him but you do.

"Have you given Rascal a bath?"

"No,"

I'm tired of taking care of him, you know that rascal loves the both of us very much, I can't wait until mom gets home.

"Why's that?"

"I miss her, she's only been gone for three hours."

I know, but it's how I'm feeling today

"Can we go outside now?"

"Yes," we can son

We have to take my sister with us, I want her to play outside too.

"Can I bring my coloring book outside with me?"

"Yes," you can.

I hope that Rascal doesn't run away, Huey dropped a crayon and Rascal ran over to it, you better watch that he doesn't eat it. He quickly grabbed the crayon, no dog you can't have it. Huey looked in the crayon box, I can't find the blue crayon, you're sister took that crayon. Don't you remember when you had to chase him down the block? Yes, I hope that it never happens again. At least you're a good runner.

"Can you teach me how to run like you someday?"

"Yes," I will teach you how when you are fifteen years old.

You should teach me now to run, let's go outside and see how nice it is outside. Huey quickly got up off the floor, were going to head downstairs and get your sister and were going outside.

"How long do you want to be outside for?"

"I want to be outside for the rest of the afternoon."

"Let's see how your sister is going to feel about that."

"What are you doing?"

"I'm just coloring and playing with Rascal."

"Would you like to go outside?"

"No," it's so hot outside, and I'm just fine staying in here in the air conditioning.

"Why do you have to drag me outside?"

"It's not fair that I have to do everything that Huey does."

Stop acting like a little princess and let's go outside, I'm not going to ask you again, I will come out.

"Can I take me teddy bear along outside with me?"

"Yes," you can, but don't drop your teddy bear on the ground outside.

If I spend a day outside with you and Huey you're going to have to promise me that you will get me a small cone of ice cream.

"You really like your ice cream don't you?"

"Yes," I do

"Is there a problem with that?"

"No," but ice cream has a lot of sugar in it.

I didn't know that, she replied you never answered me.

"Can I please have an ice cream cone?"

"Yes," you can

You're beginning to get on my nerves.

"Why must you say that to me?"

"I'm not trying to upset you, but I want to cry, you hurt my feelings."

You know that I don't like it when, you cry, I know, but it's your fault that I'm crying in the first place.

"What's it going to take to make you happy?"

I want to see you run around with the red cape on, I also want you to put on your mask.

"So if I do that, will you be happy and stop crying?"

"Yes," I will.

I don't remember where the red cape is nor the mask. I'm sure that you will be able to find everything that you need. Thank you for being so positive, It's going to take me more than a moment to go into the house, and find the cape and mask.

"How about if you and Huey wait, out on the porch?"

"We will wait there then."

It was a nice day outside, and the sun was high in the sky. It's so hot outside, it feels like its eighty-five degrees outside. At least it's not raining, and besides that Huey doesn't seem to be complaining much. He's a boy and I'm a princess. No, you're no princess, but I am.

I'm tired of arguing with you. Just leave me alone and go look for your red cape. Their dad walked back into the house and walked towards the basement.

He was feeling sad about having an argument with his kids, he thought to himself what kind of monster have I become. He was feeling down and out and he thought why did I even have kids if I'm going to treat them like crap.

He thought on and his eyes began to tear up, then the tears began to run down his face. He carefully walked down the steep steps down into his basement.

The basement was so dark that he could barely even see the steps, so he switched on the light and continued down the steep steps. Once at the bottom of the steps, he turned towards a clothing chest that he's had in his basement for several years. On top of the chest was an old wool blanket that his grandmother had made him when was just a boy.

He opened up the chest and a lot of dust came up and went into his nostrils and made him sneeze. He sneezed a few times and continued on looking through the chest for his red cape. He just couldn't come across the cape. There were some folded up t-shirts and some summer dresses.

He saw that there was a blue short sleeve shirt that had some cuts in it. As he got closer to the bottom of the chest of clothes he began to find his wife's underwear. He wasn't very happy with that and picked up the red pair of underwear and threw them out of the chest.

Chapter Two: Tasks To Do

He dug down deeper into the chest and he found an old pair of stinky socks that were probably sitting in there for many years. The socks didn't even match, and they were black and had a lot of lint on them. He couldn't take it much longer, he couldn't even find anything that came close to being a cape.

He threw the black socks aside and with his wife's underwear. He thought oh great I hope that my wife doesn't ask for these underwear again, or maybe I should just hide them. He thought on I better not keep looking through this chest of clothes.

Now he was at the bottom of the clothes chest, there were two dead stink bugs lying on their backs. He looked around for an old rag that he could use to clean up the clothes chest with.

He saw that there was an old antique lamp on a table that was right next to the chest of clothes. His elbow almost bumped into the lamp, the lamp was all dusty and had some kind of cover over the glass part of it. Sweat began to pour down his forehead, he had forgot to put on his deodorant that morning and he began to stink.

He thought to himself I can't go on stinking so bad. He stopped what he was doing in the basement and went back upstairs, but forgot to turn off the light downstairs. He walked into his master bedroom and saw the sheets on the bed needed to be washed.

There were a few wine stains on the bottom of the white sheets, he's very particular about his fancy bed sheets. He prefers to clean his sheets every Friday, his wife likes to make the occasional exception and wash the sheets every two weeks.

This really gets on his nerves and he gets into a heated discussion with her. After every argument she's always the one who's right and he's always wrong. He no longer chooses to argue with his wife, one night he was so tired from watching the kids and shampooing the carpets.

He barely even made it into the bedroom without collapsing. His wife looked at him and asked him what was the matter, he said I'm just so tired and I never want to have another long day like this one. Oh honey why don't you come over here and give me a hug and a kiss, I will do that for you beautiful.

"What's that you're eating my love?"

"I'm eating some chocolate cookies, and milk."

"Why are you eating cookies in my bed?"

"I was just hungry"

Alright after you are done eating the cookies you better not have gotten any crumbs on the bed or blankets, or you will be cleaning up the bed and washing the blankets again. I'm not in the mood to argue with you about your petty non sense.

I just wanted to eat in peace and you're making such a big deal out of me eating while in bed, you never see me eating while I'm in bed. That's true honey, but please stop picking on me and let me eat in peace. I would actually prefer if you left the room.

"Why must I leave the room?"

"You have to leave the room because I'm tired of looking at you and arguing with you."

Baby that's not right, you will have to get over it. You aren't acting like the same women that I had married.

"How could you say that?"

"I should smack you in the face for that kind of remark."

This is why our marriage is going sour. No, I don't think it's me at all. Why yes it is,

"How so?"

"You make the kids cry and you make me miserable by the way you pick on everything that I do."

I haven't criticized you at all lately, yes you have been.

"Tell me an instance when I did that?"

"Last week you told me that I made the Mac and cheese" wrong and that it was my fault for why you burned the Mac and cheese.

While standing in his bedroom he couldn't stop thinking about how him and his wife would stand in the bedroom and argue about every little thing. He walked up to his closet and flung it open, some hangers fell out onto the floor and he bent down to pick them up and he heard a stink bug flying around his room.

He happened to look up at his ceiling fan and noticed that the light inside of the ceiling fan was infested with stink bugs. One stink bug came flying down from the one blade of the ceiling fan and landed on his left shoulder. He isn't afraid of bugs and didn't seem to mind that there was a stink bug on his shoulder.

He just went on with what he was doing, one of his wife's dresses fell off of the hanger and he remembered that was her favorite dress, he knew that if he got a stain on it she would probably kill him or just yell out for an hour. He looked through his shirts and there was his red cape hiding beneath a black long sleeve sweater.

The sweater was made of wool and felt so warm against his skin. He was careful not to knock down any more of his wife's dresses. He didn't want to get, grilled on why he was going through her clothes. He was careful when touching and moving her clothes around in the closet.

He looked down at his wrist watch and realized that almost an hour had gone by and his kids were still waiting for him out in the hot sun. He went to reach for something and the smell from his under arms was so bad that he couldn't stand it. So he decided to put everything down and hop straight into the shower.

He took a nice long shower and used hot water and it made his sore knees feel much better. Suddenly he began thinking about his wife and all the arguments that they have had over the years. He thought to himself why did I even get married? What was I thinking. Then all the hot water was used up and cold water began to run down his back, he finished washing himself off with the body wash.

He made sure that he washed under his arm pits good and then washed himself down and turned the water off and opened the curtain, when he did Rascal was standing there looking at him panting from being overheated. Hi Rascal what are you doing in here? Why can't you let me to take a shower in peace.

Why must everyone be bothering me at all hours of the day? Then he heard Huey calling him, Dad my sister was hitting me and trying to throw a stick at me. Why can't you get along with your sister. Dad she won't stop being mean to me so, I left her alone and she began to cry.

I want you to not come in here, I'm in my robe and not dressed yet. Dad please let me come in anyway, It's okay I guess, come on in.

> "Did you find your red cape yet?"

> "Yes," I did, it's right here on my bed, take a good look at it, I'm going to throw it away soon.

We know that when you run around with the red cape on, it makes us so happy. You know you're strange kids,

> "Why's that?"

> "Because, normal kids, don't like when their parents run around with a silly suit on."

Dad were special and that's fine with us.

> "Why did you take a shower?"

> "I was hot and sweaty and needed to clean off the stink from my
> body."

I was stinky and you don't know just how bad the stink was. That's because your arm pit hair is too long.

> "How do you know that?"

> "Because I can see, when you wear cut off shirts."

> "Why don't you cut off your stinky under arm hair?"

> "I don't want to son"

I don't want you to tell me what to do with my life. I'm an adult and know how to care for myself, you're in another rotten mood. I'm sorry, but I just have been feeling sad lately. That's no reason to remain in a sour mood.

> "Are you going to come outside with us?"

> "Yes," I will, and you have to learn to be more patient with me.

Alexis walked into the room bleary eyed

> "What are you doing?

> "I'm just talking to Huey, then I promise that I will go outside with you."

> "I stubbed my little toe on the edge of the book shelf."

> "How did you do that?"

> "I wasn't watching and stubbed my big toe.

> "Could you please look at it?"

> "I will"

If you want me to look at it you will have to come over here. I'm no longer going to chase you kids around this big house. You really stubbed your big toe, but the good news is you will be fine.

> "How long is it going to take for it to be better?"

> "Two days, I love you but sometimes you do the dumbest things."

Try not to stub your toe again. Alright, I'm ready to run now. Alexis ran over to Rascal and began to pull on his ears and this made him cry out. Be very careful I really don't think that he likes his ears pulled like that. But I'm just playing with him.

"How would you like it if someone pulled on your ears?"

"I wouldn't like it."

You know how he feels about it, all I want to do is play fetch with Rascal but he doesn't seem interested in doing that with me. Maybe you upset him or something. No, I know that Rascal isn't upset with me.

Let's go, Mr. Ruffalo took Alexis and Huey outside and Rascal came along. The sun is so bright dad yeah I know but you will get used to it I'm sure. I would like to go camping again.

"Why do you want to go camping again?"

"I like nature and helping you to build a camp fire."

"It costs a lot of money to keep going on camping trips."

"What do you think of camping?"

"Alexis said I don't like nature."

"I would rather stay home and play with Rascal."

"Can you tell me what you don't like about nature?"

"I don't like all the bugs that come out and buzz around me."

You know what, you're so much like your mom, she doesn't like bugs either and likes to be treated like a princess. I'm a little princess, I know that.

"Would you like to make s'mores tonight?"

"That sounds great dad, and asked his daughter how does that sound to you?"

"I don't feel like eating marshmallows"

"Why do you have to be so difficult?"

"I don't know dad you know how I am."

Then a cricket came hoping past Alexis and she made a sour face and looked down at the cricket and watched it then bent down and then squished it with her flip flop.

"Why did you have to squish the cricket?"

"I don't like bugs and I like to kill them with my flip flops."

Meanwhile Huey began to wonder around and headed towards the side of the house. The neighbor was sitting out on his porch on an old rocking chair. Right next to him he had a small wooden table and there was a beer can sitting there. The man pulled out a pack of cigarettes and began to smoke. Huey didn't like what this man was doing.

"What's this man doing over here?"

"He's smoking a cigarette."

"What's a cigarette?"

It's something that you can smoke. It really stinks, I know, he shouldn't be smoking so close to us.

"Do you think I should have a talk with him?"

"Yes," I think that you should.

Wait here and I will be right back, Hi Mr. Crawler

"How are you doing today?"

"I'm doing fine"

"What do you want to talk about?"

"Let's talk about your habits"

"Is my smoking bothering you?"

"Yes," it is.

I don't appreciate you letting your cigarette butts around the bushes at the front of my house. I'm sorry, and you know that I have two little kids. I understand what your trying to say to me.

If you don't stop littering I'm going to call the Police. Don't threaten me like that. let's take care of the problem like the men we are. I tell you what, I'm trying to quit smoking and that should end our little disagreement. Tomorrow if I come out and see just one more cigarette butt I will be back here and things are going to change.

"Do you understand me?"

"Yes," I do.

I have to go back to watching my kids, okay. I wish that we could have talked more though, I will be back over when I put my kids in for a nap.

"Would you like a beer?"

"No," thank you.

"How comes your wife isn't here to watch the kids?"

"She's at work and by the way what do you do all day, just sit here."

I have been retired for close to twenty years now. By looking at your front lawn I can tell you don't like to cut your grass, no, I don't like to cut it. I would rather just call my cousin and have him cut it while I sit here and drink beers all afternoon.

"What are you going to do when the summer is over?"

"I don't know"

"I'm thinking about moving down to Texas."

"How soon were you thinking of doing that?"

"I haven't thought about that yet."

Alright Mr. Ruffalo you have asked me so many questions and I can't not even remember all the questions. I got to go now. Try to remember what I discussed with you. I will, bye now.

"Mr. Crawler stood up and walked inside."

"What is it?"

"Alexis was playing around with Rascal in the back yard and Rascal fell on his side and is having trouble breathing."

"Where's Alexis?"

"She's lying by his side, and is talking to him."

She keeps on telling him that it's going to be okay and she won't leave his side. Let me take a look and I will call the traveling vet if I have to. Mom should be back in an hour.

Thank goodness dad. Now show me what's going on with Rascal. It seems like Rascal's getting old and tired. I wish he would get up and play fetch with me outside.

Just let him rest, don't push him or make him get up. I can tell that he's over heated and is really panting, don't worry he'll perk up when we go back inside the house.

"Are you sure?"

"Yes," I'm sure.

"Why don't you still call the vet?"

"Because she will just tell me to let him rest inside the cool house."

"Hot weather isn't good for dogs,"

"Why's that?"

"Because dogs have so much fur on their body and it causes them to get warmer quicker than us while outside."

"What are you doing?"

"Get out of the mud puddle in the yard."

You know I like to play in the mud. Son I don't like it when you get all dirty, I'm going to have to take you and give you a bath. I like to take baths, you never said that before, don't wander away too far from us. I don't want you near the busy street.

"Didn't you hear about the little girl that got hit in the street last week?"

"No"

"What was her name?"

"I don't remember what her name was"

"Was it Emily?"

"No," her name wasn't Emily; I think it was Sara.

"Why must you argue with me?"

"I don't know, I'm just not in a cheery mood."

He saw that his wife was pulling in the driveway, Look whose home, we love our mom. Huey and Alexis came running up to the car.

"Hey mom how are you doing?"

"I'm doing good kids"

"How are the both of you feeling?"

"We feel okay, but our dad is being grumpy today."

"Why's that?"

"He just hasn't played with us like he used to. I see, how about you let me get of my car and I will start cooking."

What are you going to make for dinner tonight? I'm going to make spaghetti and meatballs and for desert I got a double chocolate cake, but you two have to share the cake among yourselves.

"How was work?"

"It was good, but now I'm tired and want to spend my time with you guys."

I heard that you weren't playing with the kids today. No, I'm not feeling myself lately, oh honey you will be okay, I think that you need to go get more counseling tonight. I don't want to, tough, I need to practice tough love with you. I want all of you to follow me into the kitchen. I'm going to put you all to work, no pushing and keep your hands away from the stove.

"Yes," mom

"What can I do to help honey?"

"You can just stand behind me and observe."

"Why can't I help cook, because when you tried to cook before you almost burned down the house."

It wasn't that bad, your making things up, I want you to take a paper towel and wipe down the counter top then we will start cooking. Were so hungry.

"What time are we going to eat?"

"We are going to eat at six o clock"

That's so far away mom oh quit your whining, if I can wait so can the three of you.

"What are you doing honey?"

"I was just looking for some bread."

Let the bread go honey, I will make the garlic bread this time. Why don't you go to the grocery store, we need another loaf of Italian bread.

"Why must I always go to the grocery store?"

"That's because I'm busy cooking here"

"Why don't you take Huey and Alexis along with you?"

"No," we would rather stay here and not go with.

Why don't you just go with your dad. Besides that, dad doesn't like to go to the grocery store alone. No, it's okay kids if you don't want to go then you don't have to, I'm going to leave now,

I should be back soon. Hurry back, you don't want to miss dinner. Mr. Ruffalo walked over to the shelf at the front door and grabbed his wife's car keys and rushed out the door.

"So have you been behaving yourself and staying out of the mud?"

"No," I haven't mom,

I was a bad boy, then I should make you sit in the corner. No, I'm too old for that, no you're not and you better watch your mouth. I might wash your mouth out with soap, if you don't start listening to me.

Alright, then I will start listening to you better. Your sister, is more behaved then you have ever been. See Alexis is helping me and you're just standing there staring at me.

"What would you like me to do mom?"

"I want you to help get the oven prepped."

You know how to help mom get the stove prepared for cooking. I want you to open up the cabinet by the stove and take out a nice big glass bowl. Hold on and let me grab the bowl.

If you drop the bowl I'm going to put you in time out. I will be careful. You better be careful or else, Huey took his time and carefully grabbed the bowl. Now that's good, now set the bowl down on the countertop to the left side of the stove.

"What's next?"

"That was a good job, I want you to pick out what kind of spaghetti noodles you would like with your meal."

You and Alexis figure out what kind of noodles you would like. Huey slowly opened the door to the cubort and him and Alexis looked in.

They were looking at the three different kinds of spaghetti noodles. There are too many to choose from, oh stop it just make a choice and then come over here again and help me. Mom Alexis and I are done.

"Which ones did you choose?"

"We chose the thick noodles, alright bring them over here then."

As Huey went to pick up the container of spaghetti, it opened up and spaghetti noodles fell out over the floor. Look at what you did Huey, I'm going to make you pick them up. Come on mom, you made the mess so it's your job to clean it up.

"Why can't my sister help me to clean up the mess?"

"Because you made the mess, now clean it up now or I will put you in time out for ten minutes."

Mom I will, Huey walked over to the back wall of the living room and picked up the little broom and dust pan. He slowly walked over with the dust pan and broom and began to carefully sweep up the spaghetti. That's a good job, keep doing the job.

"How comes you aren't cooking yet?"

"We have to wait until dad gets back from the grocery store."

"Why can't we use the spaghetti that I dropped on the floor?"

"It fell on the floor and is no good anymore, that's such a waste of food."

"Don't you think that Rascal would like to eat it?"

"No," he doesn't like to eat spaghetti.

“Has anyone seen him for the past half an hour?”

“No,” we haven't

“Did my you let him back inside the house.”

“No,” we didn't, you kids are so careless

What if he wanders into the street and gets killed because you two don't seem to care. I do, no you don't, if you really loved him then you wouldn't have left him outside in the heat.

I want you to go the front door right now and see if Rascal is there. Alright I will. Alexis took off running towards the front door, I said no running, fine, then I won't run.

Alexis made a silly face at her, then stuck her tongue out and said you can't catch me Huey. Stop trying to get Huey all wound up, and silly. Alexis pulled the door open and there was no sign of Rascal. Mom he's not there.

That means were going to have walk around the neighborhood and find him again. No, that's not true but it is. I'm in no mood to put on my sneakers and run a mile looking for him.

“How about when dad gets home he looks for him?”

“That sounds like a good idea.”

“Hey mom what are you doing with the dish rag?”

“I'm going to wash it, it stinks like yesterday's dinner.”

You know what mom you are so particular about where everything is kept in this house. There's a reason for it, there's a reason why I make you and Huey clean your rooms every day. If I wouldn't there would be stink bugs living in the house.

“Why must you bring up those stink bugs?”

“Because the stink bugs like a stinky house and this house isn't stinky.”

Besides that, the floor of this kitchen is filthy and it needs to be moped.

“Who's going to help mom to mop the kitchen floor?”

“I will.”

I will show you where I keep the cleaning supplies.

"Come with me, alright mom here's the cleaning stuff?"

"The keep the cleaning stuff in my bedroom bathroom."

Don't mess up my cleaning supply closet, or you will have to take everything out and clean it.

"Is that understood?"

"Yes," it is.

After you're done mopping the floor you can go in the living room and watch your silly shows. Mom that sounds good, meanwhile Alexis and I are going to check in the pantry to see if we have enough spaghetti sauce for tonight's dinner.

"Mom?"

"Yes"

"What's the matter?"

There are two dead stink bugs lying in the bucket that the mops in, and there's some stinky black water in the bottom of the bucket. I have to hold my nose it stinks so much mom. Here let me have it and I will dump the black water in the yard and while I'm doing that, I will take a good look around for Rascal.

Laura took the bucket and ran to the front door and walked out, I'm tired of how mom is making us do all this work while dad's away. I think that we should think about running away from here.

"Why?"

"We couldn't survive out on the streets. But don't you want to go on an adventure?"

No, and I would rather stay here. Okay party pooper, then we won't run away then. You don't have it that bad Huey, our parents care about us and feed us well. There's no need to run away.

You better be moping the kitchen floor or no ice cream or cake tonight. I still cannot find Rascal, but I have good news your dad is pulling into the driveway. He didn't look too happy either.

"Is he coming in here?"

"Yes," your dad will be in.

"There he is now"

"Hi dad how are you?"

"It's a long story kids."

"Please tell us about it?"

"As long as everyone is going to listen to me."

Chapter Four: Odds & Ends

I get to the store, then I get out of the car and I see that on the street ahead of me was some yellow crime scene tape. I happened to look over and I saw an elderly man who could barely even walk.

He walked over to the grocery store and tripped right at the entrance, and began to yell out some cuss words and there were children standing around with their parents watching the whole thing unfolding.

I stood back and watched too, then I thought to myself I better do something to help this man. When I approached him he tried to hit me with his cane so I quickly had to back away.

He didn't say anything to anyone and was just a mean old man, I stepped around him and went on shopping. Once inside the grocery store I looked back and saw that there was an ambulance that just pulled up.

The old man yelled out I hate people, and there was a young EMT guy standing right by him. The man told the elderly man to calm down, but instead he yelled out another cuss word and then afterwards kept his mouth shut. The one mom couldn't stand how this elderly man was talking and told him to be quiet in a stern way and it worked.

"That was a long story"

"What else happened?"

"There was a kid in the store that kept on running around knocking down stuff from the shelfs."

"Did you say anything to him?"

"No"

I saw that his mom was in the isle next door. I walked over to her and I said you better take control of your kid, he's knocking things off of the shelves. She acted like she didn't hear me, and nodded her head. She had the look of disgust on her face, her hair was long and she didn't seem to care in the least bit.

"Did you say anything else to her?"

"No," I didn't

I didn't even want to look at her again.

"Did you see anyone else in the grocery store?"

"Yes," but I didn't talk to them.

The cashier that rang me up wasn't very good at math and couldn't give me the right amount of change, back. I was feeling flustered but I had to be patient with her. I was going to help her, but I figured that I would just let her go.

"Why didn't you help her dad?"

"She didn't ask for my help."

You're such a good child, and have good manners, thank you. However, you haven't been a good boy, I just like to have fun. Yes, you do, but you also have to listen to us, after all we are your parents.

Don't give mom a hard time, she been through a lot this past week at work. Let's get dinner ready, Lauren began to boil the water in the pan where she was going to cook the noodles.

"Hey Hun could you please grab me the extra thick noodles from the pantry?"

"Sure I will"

"How many boxes of noodles would you like?"

"I would like two please."

We have one box of noodles left.

While you are over there, grab me a jar of spaghetti sauce. The jar of spaghetti sauce is on the top shelf and it's hard for me to reach all the way up there. Stop being so dramatic honey, I wasn't trying to be.

"Would you like me to get it?"

"No"

Mr. Ruffalo reached up and his left hand slipped off the jar. The jar of sauce came crashing down and landed on his foot. He jumped up and let out an groan, while the glass jar of sauce shattered and the red sauce was now all over his shoe and was running down the sides of his shoe. He was wearing a nice pair of Nike sneakers, and couldn't believe what had just happened.

He ran over to the sink and grabbed a whole roll of paper towels, and reached down and picked up the broom and when. He was bending down to reach for the dust pan, Lauren didn't seem him there and walked back into him and dropped the aluminum foil and it fell into the glass bowl. You're lucky I didn't have anything breakable in my hands.

I was right behind you, and why didn't you say so honey? I thought you were busy and I didn't want to disturb you. No, now let me continue on with my cooking. I got sauce all over my left shoe.

"How did that happen?"

"My hand just slipped off of the jar as I was reaching for it and we'll it just came crashing down and landed directly on my foot."

Huey and Alexis were standing idle while Mr. Ruffalo had to clean up the mess. Hey kids why don't you help your father to clean up the remaining mess, we did enough today, you had us mop the floors.

You're lucky I didn't make you dust all around all of the window frames. Maybe I should do that next time. Son can you please go to the sink and wet a paper towel for me? I sure will, just give me a moment. Huey went to walk over to the sink and almost tripped over his untied shoes.

The long lace was hanging over the side of his shoe. He took a minute and bent down to tie both of his shoes. While he was bent down Lauren didn't seem him and again almost tripped over him. Look before you walk mom, you almost walked into me. I have had enough with not having enough room in the kitchen.

Huey and Alexis I want the both of you to go into the living room right now. And you too honey. But wait I'm still cleaning up the floor and my shoe. I don't care, what you're doing, just get out of the kitchen and join the kids in the living room.

"Why are you acting so mean?"

"I'm not trying to act mean, it's just I'm busy trying to cook and don't need to trip over anyone and break my neck."

I understand what you mean honey, but I feel bad when I'm not helping you. I tell you what you can do awhile honey, go out in the neighborhood and look for Rascal. He has probably run away into the neighbor's yard and you need to run after him and find him before he gets hit by a car.

"You're so demanding today"

"What's going on with you?"

"Nothing is going on with me."

I'm just tired of things not getting down around here. Alright like what, like you haven't dusted for a week.

"I was busy, doing what?"

"I was watching the kids and trying to be nice to the neighbor."

"What's going on with the neighbor?"

"You know Mr. Crawler?"

"Yes," he has been smoking his cigarettes and throwing the empty cigarette butts in our front yard.

"What's the matter with him?"

"I don't know but I confronted him about it and he said that he was planning on stopping smoking."

"What did he say?"

That's about it, but I threatened him that I was going to call the Police and have them come in and have a talk with him.

"What did he say after that?"

"His jaw just dropped and he didn't have anything to say."

Alright times a wasting, you need to go now to look for Rascal or you will never find him. Wow you're so negative today, no I'm not, it's the truth. He could be in the next county by now, you know how fast he can run. Now stop whining and go get the dog.

Alexis and Huey love Rascal and don't want him to get hurt. There's a good change he's wandering along on the street not knowing of the immediate dangers of cars. The kids will stay here and wait for you.

I tell you what I'm getting tired of this. It's your own fault you're the one that left him out then forgot about him. Let's stop playing the blame game and I will be back, Mr. Ruffalo ran out to the front door and slammed the door behind him.

"Hey mom?"

"Yes,"

"Do you think Rascal will be okay'?"

"He's going to live now don't you worry you little princess of mine."

"How soon before dinner is done?"

"It will be another half an hour."

"When do you think that dad's going to be back?"

"He will probably be back in an hour or two if he finds him and he probably will."

"You know mom, you are a good cook, thank you."

"How about you?"

"Do you think I'm a good cook?"

"Yes," you are, but dad's funny when he cooks.

"How so?"

"He doesn't know how to cook well and always ends up burning the food."

I laugh at him when he goes to cook. No, Huey you're being mean to your dad, don't laugh at him, he's trying to do his best to help out around here. Just tell him that he does a good job even when he doesn't.

I will listen to you and do that. Now you're being a good boy, and stay in the living with Alexis until I'm done cooking. I'm worried about dad, he's fine. I don't want him to get hurt while chasing Rascal.

He's a grown man and knows how to deal with situations that he may find himself in. I understand that but what if a car would veer off of the road and hit him.

"Why would your dad be on the road on the first place?"

"Rascal could be running down the road."

"No," I don't think that he's running down the road.

Besides that, he likes to eat, and probably wandered into the neighbor's yard, and is begging for food. I hope you're right about that mom. I don't want old Rascal to become road pizza. He won't, don't worry yourself about it, he's just a dog that's always hungry and looking for food.

He's special to Alexis and I, I want you and Alexis to sit on the couch and stay there until I'm done cooking and your dad gets back. I don't want to hear another word until I'm done cooking. It takes a lot of concentration for me to cook dinner. Mom we want to go outside and run around the yard.

"What are you going to do?"

"We just want to sit outside."

Alright go ahead but be careful, I will be watching you both from the kitchen window.

"You have to play nice with her"

"Can you promise me that you will?"

"I will mom, you may go."

Huey and Alexis opened the front door and walked out. Huey closed the door behind them. Once they got outside the hot sun and humidity hit them. It made Alexis feel sluggish.

Let's go and run around. I don't want to run though, oh come on stop acting like a princess and play in the mud with me. I'm going to stand here and watch you play in the mud. You're such a party pooper. I'm tired of being around you Huey, I'm tired of you too Alexis.

Tears began to run down the both sides of Alexis and she tripped over a rock and fell onto the ground. She remained crying, you are such a bully. No I'm not, I want to go tell mom what you said to me.

Don't be a mommy baby, I'm a mommy baby and there's nothing that you can do about it. I want to go tell mom right now, all of sudden Lauren opened the kitchen window and said is everyone behaving. Mom, yes, Huey's a mean bully.

Lauren's smile immediately left her face and a frown face went on. Now listen what did I tell you about bullying your sister. Stop bullying her right now or else. I'm sorry, I won't speak to her then for the rest of the day. Go on with what you two were doing and let me cook, or I will have dad come home and discipline you both.

"Is that what you two want?"

"No," it's not

Just relax and cut the drama and act like kids should act. Lauren went back to cooking and left the kids play, I wonder when dad's going to get home? I don't know but I'm getting worried about Rascal, I hope he's okay and happy.

"What do you think is above the clouds?"

"I don't really know, I haven't thought about that."

"Would you like to travel into space someday?"

"No," I'm not interested in space exploration at all.

"I would rather swim in the open ocean."

"How about you Alexis?"

"I want to go to space someday and check it out."

"You're so much braver then I ever will be."

"Where's your sense of adventure?"

"It left me"

"Why?"

"I would rather see my parents happy, then making my own self happy."

In some ways Huey is a good boy, but there are times when you can be a real stinker. That's true, I hear some sirens. Let's go check out where they are coming from. Let's go, so they ran around to the side of the house and saw that there was an officer who pulled up in a Police car. He looked out the window and saw Huey and Alexis.

"What are you doing on this fine afternoon?"

"We are just walking around the back yard playing in the mud."

"How are you doing this evening officer?"

"I'm doing okay"

"Do you know why I'm here?"

"No"

I was called here two hours ago, and the person wouldn't tell me their name right away, I had to keep asking the individual their name. His name is Mr. Crawler and he said to me that your dad was threatening and harassing him all afternoon.

"Were you there?"

"Yes," but I didn't hear what was said.

I'm going to go talk to your mother then. Alright just be careful if you're going to play out in the street. No, officer we don't play out in the street and we don't have a basketball to play with. I found an old basketball in the alley the other day.

"Would you like it?"

"Then come and get it."

The officer opened the trunk of his car and pulled out the basketball and gently handed it to Huey. Thank you so much officer, you're welcome, now have a good. Huey and Alexis looked at each other and said what kind of trouble did dad get himself into this time? You know what, I hope that dad comes home later tonight so that he doesn't need to talk to the officer.

I agree with you Huey. Meanwhile Mr. Ruffalo still was walking down the block, he was now almost out of the county. His short sleeve shirt was all covered in sweat, and his arms were burning from the hot sun beading down on them.

He was just about out of breath, and his knees were beginning to want to lock up on him. So luckily there was a bench nearby and he took a seat. He thought to himself so far I have looked in every neighbor's yard and still no sign of Rascal, then he thought on, oh no what if he did get hit by a car.

He stood back up and could feel that his heart was beating a mile a minute and the sweat was just pouring down his forehead. He thought to himself I should have put on a head ban and my funny looking red cape to make the kids in the neighborhood laugh. As he was walking along a black bird flew over him and took a crap and it landed on his shirt.

Oh man what did I do to deserve this? He kept on walking, the bird crap really stank and he could barely stand it. As he was walking along he accidently stepped on the cat's tail who was walking on a leash right in front of him. The cat let out a scream and the owner of the cat looked back at Mr. Ruffalo.

"Sir. what did you do to my cat?"

"I just stepped on your cat's tail."

I'm sorry for stepping on your cat's tail. It's okay Sir, just keep walking. Mr. Ruffalo looked through his pocket, and noticed that he had forgot his smart phone. He wiped the sweat from his forehead, with his right hand.

All of a sudden he came upon an alley, and there was a lot of trash in the alley way. A man on a motorcycle, drove through the alley at a high rate of speed. He was going over the speed limit and almost crashed into a trash can that was at the end of the alley.

There was a stray cat walking along aimlessly among the trash cans. The cat was missing some of its fur and had so many whiskers on its face. He was an ugly gray and black color.

He had an ugly short tail, that looked like part of it was bit off. He walked over closer to the alley and saw that the one trash can was overfilled with trash.

The one trash bag had a big rip in the side. Some trash was falling out of the bag. It looked like there was an old moldy cake on the ground in front of the trash can. Mr. Ruffalo almost threw up after seeing the cake. He leaned over and felt like he was going to throw up.

Chapter Five: The Outing

Suddenly he saw Rascal come running up to him. Rascal had a scratch on his upper lip and was whimpering. You'll be okay buddy, he let out another whimper, buddy I feel bad for you. Let's go home. Rascal carefully walked down the sidewalk with Mr. Ruffalo.

Mr. Ruffalo was just about out of breath, but kept walking on anyway. As Mr. Ruffalo walked along the sidewalk with Rascal, he happened to look off to his left and saw a nice little shop. The shop had a large bay window and there were things lined up along the inside of the window.

In big bold letters it said today only, we are having a big sale on different types of fabric. There was another big sign and written on that sign it said come on in and take a look around. A young fellow came walking over by the window and began to clean the window.

The young fellow had a smile on his face and this made Mr. Ruffalo smile. Rascal was walking around in a circle and watching as some people walked by. A young women walked past and kneeled down and was ready to pet Rascal.

"What's your name?"

"My name is Susie and I want to pet your dog,"

"Do you mind?"

"No," I don't mind go right ahead and pet him.

"How old is your dog?"

"He's nine years old yet."

"What's his name?"

His name is Rascal; I think that name fits him just fine.

"What are you doing today Mister?"

"You don't have to call me Mister, my name is Mr. Ruffalo.

"No," I prefer to call you mister.

"Where are your parents Susie?"

"They are over there shopping for wine at the liquor store."

I have to get home soon Susie, so finish up petting Rascal and I will talk to you later. It was nice to meet your dog mister, have a good rest of the night, you too Mister.

The sky was now dark and Mr. Ruffalo looked up and saw some bright stars. He was careful not to let go of Rascals collar, Rascal kept on trying to pull away from him. Sit down, I had enough of you trying to get away from me. I don't know why you won't listen to me today.

Mr. Ruffalo looked down at Rascal, and he was panting. Rascal began to wag his tail and let out a bark at Mr. Ruffalo. I'm sure you wanna play fetch. Rascal barked again. Be quiet, I've already petted you like five times, an old lady walked past and began to laugh.

"What's so funny Ma'am?"

"You're so funny, I've never saw anyone talk to their dog before."

Why don't you just keep on walking. I will Sir. and I hope you and your conversation with your dog. Mr. Ruffalo looked at the little shop in front of him. The shop sign said no dogs are allowed inside at any time.

Listen Rascal, I want you to sit here while I quickly run into the shop, if you run away one more time I won't be looking for you. I'm tired and want to enjoy my time while I'm in this shop. Now please stay here until I come out. As he walked over to the shops door, Rascal turned his head and looked at him.

You're being a good boy Rascal, and Mr. Ruffalo walked over and carefully opened the shops door. The door had a bell on it, and it made a nice little sound. The inside of the shop smelled like strawberry candles. Mr. Ruffalo looked over to the left side of the shop and there were rows of hangers with old shirts hung over them.

Some of the old shirts had rips in them, and had various stains on them. To the right of him there was a large shelf that was below the large bay window. There were some bobble head dolls and Barbie dolls that were sitting on the shelf. There were some other various nic nacs on the shelf. There was a small vase with fake plants in it.

The vase had a little orange sticker on it and was marked to be ten dollars. Mr. Ruffalo wasn't sure why he had come into the shop. There was little old women standing behind the counter, she had a pained look on her face. She was all hunched over and looked to be in distress.

"Ma'am are you okay?"

"I'm doing okay Sir."

I'm just recovering from falling down the steps at home.

"How many steps did you fall down?"

"I don't remember that Sir."

"Are you looking for anything special?"

"No," not really, I was just browsing around.

If there's anything you need then, just let me know. I will Ma'am, he walked around the back of the shop and there were some necklaces and lamps for sale. There was an old antique lamp, and the bulb in the lamp was broken. On an end stand there was a few hot wheel cars. Each car was marked with an orange, sticker.

Each car was marked as a dollar, there were so many to choose from. The hot wheel's cars were cool looking and Mr. Ruffalo thought to himself well maybe Huey might want a hot wheel's car. As he was walking along a little cricket crawled out, from a hole in the floor, the cricket crawled beneath his foot.

He stepped down and the poor little cricket got crushed below his foot. He felt bad for the little cricket and went on browsing through the store. A nice silver necklace caught his eye and he took a good look at it, but decided not to buy it. He saw a red cape and a black mask with eye holes in it.

There was a tag that was hanging down, it said four dollars and he thought that it was a perfect, price. He reached into his left pants pocket and pulled out his wallet. He went through his wallet and discovered a hundred-dollar bill.

His eyes lit up and he had a big smile on his face. He looked at the mask and it too had an orange price tag on it. The price tags said five dollars, he thought well that price isn't so bad. He picked up the cape and mask and took it over to the women.

"Are you done shopping?"

"Yes," I'm done shopping,

"Are you going to pay with cash or credit?"

"I'm going to pay with, cash today."

He quickly pulled out his wallet, and gave her the cash, and walked away towards the door. Rascal was still sitting there patiently. Good boy Rascal, you listened well tonight.

Mr. Ruffalo carefully put on the red cape and the black mask. He forgot to take the takeoff of the cape, so the price tag hung down and was lying on the black dirty street. The smile still remained on his face, he was feeling good about himself and marched on while holding onto Rascal.

Cars were passing by so quickly, that caused his cape to get all blown around. As he kept on walking forward he almost tripped over the cape because of how long it was. All of a sudden Rascal stopped and raised his leg, and peed on the yellow fire hydrant.

Must you pee on everything on our way back? Mr. Ruffalo walked past a large metal bench, and there were three people sitting on the bench, they all looked to be in there, late seventies. The one man was holding his cane and the man next to him was wearing a wind breaker jacket. The three elderly men weren't smiling but frowning.

So Mr. Ruffalo stood in front of them and spun around, this made all three of them smile and laugh. The one elderly man pointed his finger at him and laughed. All of a sudden he began to cough and almost fell over onto the man next to him.

Mr. Ruffalo was happy that he could make them feel better, there was a puddle of water by the street where he was standing. A bus came close to the sidewalk and passed by very quickly and some water splashed up and hit Mr. Ruffalo and Rascal this made the old men laugh some more.

Mr. Ruffalo made a grumpy look but the old men were still laughing. Then an old women came walking along with a Christmas sweater on and was wearing lit up sneakers.

"Hey Ma'am how are you doing this evening?"

"I'm doing good young man"

"What's your doggies name?"

"His name is Rascal"

"Can I pet him?"

"You sure can"

"Why are you wearing that silly red cape and black mask for?"

"I'm a super hero and are saving this town from trouble. Oh you are so funny Sir."

"Do you always walk around at night wearing a red cape and black mask?"

"No"

I just do it to make people laugh, laugher is such a good thing for people who are having a rough go of things in their lives. Sir you're a good man and they need more people like you around here, I agree with that Ma'am.

Have a good night Sir, you too. Mr. Ruffalo was feeling so happy inside and felt like he was on top of the world. Rascal kept on walking but because of the heat kept on panting. It's okay Rascal we are almost home.

Mr. Ruffalo thought maybe I can cheer up one more person before I go home tonight. On the left side of the road there was a teenage boy who was riding a bike. He happened to look over at Mr. Ruffalo and laughed and when he turned to look forward he crashed his bike into the light pole. He was lying on the ground and picked his bike back up and stood up once again.

"Are you okay kid?"

"I'm doing okay Sir?"

"Thanks for asking though. Nice red cape Sir and I love your black mask."

"Who are you going to entertain tonight?"

"Anyone I can."

You're a funny man Sir, but keep on wearing that funny red cape and people will love you. Thank you, young man. Meanwhile back at the house, so officer is our neighbor going to press charges on us? No, but this is a warning. Don't let your husband back over near the neighbor.

I will have to press charges, Okay officer, I'm sorry that my husband upset you. No, Ma'am he didn't upset me, he upset the neighbor. I'm going to get going and I will see you later take care. Have a good night, you too bye now.

"Mom what happened now?"

"The officer just wanted to talk to me."

"About what?"

"About dad."

Hey look there's our dad, the officer quickly pulled out and drove down the road. Dad, you are back, and I'm wearing my red cape. Dad you look so good in your red cape again, Rascal's looking good and happy.

"Where did you find him?"

"I found him in the alley."

"How far did you have to walk?"

"I don't know, but mom is waiting patiently for you inside."

Dad the Police showed up and talked to mom.

> "Do you know what about?"

> "No," we don't.

Go inside and talk to mom about it, Alexis couldn't stop petting Rascal, oh Rascal I missed you so much.

> "Where have you been Rascal?"

> "Rascal kept on panting and his tongue was hanging out. Come on Rascal let's get inside and cool off."

Mr. Ruffalo still had on his black mask and red cape. Although the red cape smelled like city water.

> "Hey honey, how are you tonight?"

> "I'm tired."

> "Why do you have on that silly red cape and black mask?"

> "I was making people laugh while I was walking down the street."

The kids just told me that there was a Police officer here about twenty minutes ago. Yes, and what did he want. He wanted to tell me that Mr. Crawler called him and told the officer that you were on his property harassing him.

That's not true at all, listen honey you have to be careful what you say to people. I know but I didn't mean to do anything wrong to that man.

> "How can he even say that about me?"

> "I don't know honey but you just have to be careful."

It's not good for the kids to see the Police coming over here. I know and that's the last time that I will talk to him. I now refuse to talk to him, everyone these days are so quick to blame one another. I wish things in this world would change for the better.

I know honey, but it's how the world is now. Let's get on with dinner and then we can relax with kids later. I don't feel like relaxing, I want to make things right with the neighbor.

Maybe if I look all silly and can cheer him up, maybe he will drop the charges against me. Yes but the officer didn't say that he was going to charge you. It's just a warning, oh I didn't know that. Mr. Crawler hasn't put any charges on you.

That's a good thing and I feel like a terrible person for what happened. You cannot let an old man get you down. He's just grumpy and wants to make you upset. Now we have two great kids, think of them and play with them. Every time that you play with them you have a big smile on your face.

Huey and Alexis is sitting in the living room waiting for you. Now go in there and run around, them. They will laugh and that will make you feel better. You're right that's what I'm going to do.

> "Hey dad?"

> "What are you doing?"

> "I'm going to run around and cheer both of you up."

I'm going to pretend that I'm superman, now come on kids let's go on an adventure. I'm going to spin around and act like a goofy super hero. You're spinning around too fast and are probably going to fall over. Let's see which of us gets dizzy first.

Alexis couldn't take it anymore and collapsed onto the ground and Huey and there father tripped over her leg and fell onto their backs. You're so silly and make us both laugh, please smile for us. No, kids I don't feel like smiling, I feel like everything bad that's happened to us is because of me.

Please don't worry, we love you so much and don't like to see you sad. I'm depressed, and I can't get my mind cleared of bad thoughts. Then were going to tickle you, Yes, kids but I'm not going to laugh.

Huey climbed onto his father's chest, and began to try to tickle his ears and nose. I forgot how heavy you were getting. Let me lift you up over my head Huey, you know I don't like that, but I want to lift you up to see if I still can. You can lift me up, but don't let go of me or else.

Chapter Six: Togetherness

Come over here, and play with Huey and I. Dad I don't like to come over and climb on you, I would rather just stay back and watch you and my brother play with each other. You're my daughter and I want to play silly super hero games with you. Alright dad please stop holding me up, just let me go or I will tell mom on you.

The kids opened up the toy chest, and brought out a few toy dinosaurs. The T-Rex is my favorite dinosaur, my dinosaur is better than yours. My dinosaur has horns but yours doesn't, must you kids always argue over who has the best dinosaur all of the time? No.

You two must play nice with one another, the dog came running over and grabbed one of the toy dinosaurs in his mouth. Their dad ran after the dog, get back here Rascal. Eventually he caught up with the dog and got the toy back, and returned to the living room.

"What's that face for kids?"

"Were getting hungry for dinner and would like to eat."

You're such demanding children today

"What's going on with you?"

"Nothing is going on with me."

My stomach is going to be grumbling soon if I don't eat.

"Why's Alexis sitting like that?"

"She likes to sit like that "

"Why's she starring at the wall?"

"I don't know."

"Why don't you ask her what she's looking at?"

"Hey Alexis what are you looking at?"

"I'm looking for my imaginary friend."

I didn't know that you have an imaginary friend sister, I do and I talk to him on a daily basis. I want our daughter to say grace tonight at dinner, I'm so hungry and just want to eat.

"How many of pieces of garlic bread can you eat?"

"I would like two pieces of bread."

If I give you two pieces of bread you better eat them, I will eat them.

> "How many meat balls can you eat?"

> "I just want two meat balls."

Last time you asked for two meat balls and only ate one, but dad I'm really hungry.

> "How many meat balls can you eat tonight?"

> "I just want one meat ball."

> "Are you sure?"

> "That's not much."

> "Are you and dad going to make a salad?"

> "No," we weren't planning on it.

> "Dad I think we should eat more salads."

> "Who told you that?"

> "Nobody did, I just want to try to eat healthier."

Alright kids it's time to go into the kitchen and eat dinner. Huey and Alexis and their dad walked into the dining room, and sat down in the black leather chairs. There were two lit candles in the center of the table and there were matching placemats to go around. Hey kids what would you like to drink with dinner?

> "Can we please have some lemonade?"

> "No," we just ran out of lemonade today.

I'm going to have to give you kids some green tea, we don't like green tea, then you two can have some orange soda.

> "Aren't you going to sit down at the table with us mom?"

> "Yes," I will as soon as I get the orange soda poured into the two glasses.

Their father stood up and walked over to the oven and took out the garlic from the oven. Then he took the noodles and meat balls and began to serve them. I want the both of you kids to come over here and get your plates. Why can't you just bring out plates over here or you won't be eating dinner.

I cannot put up with your childish games, stop wasting time and come over here. Huey and Alexis came over and picked up their plates and slowly walked back to the table and sat down.

"Dad my belly is bothering me"

"How does it feel?"

"It just keeps on grumbling and I have an aching pain below my belly button."

Don't worry about it, it's going to pass.

"Dad is there some kind of medicine that I can take to make my belly feel better?"

"Yes," I can give you some tums

"Why did you have to wait for us all to sit down to tell me that your stomach hurts?"

"I don't know."

Oh stop picking on Huey honey, he doesn't mean to interrupt our dinner. Let's just say grace now and eat. Let's all hold hands and say grace.

"Who's going to start praying?"

"I will, okay Alexis then let's get started."

"Are you ready to say grace?"

"Alright now start"

Dear God thank you for the great food and thank you for my family, amen. That was well done, now tomorrow night Huey will be saying grace. I want you kids to learn good family traditions. You kids have good manners and it's because we taught you well.

"How do you like the dinner?"

"It's so good and red spaghetti sauce was running down the side of his chin."

Huey was wearing a nice white short sleeve shirt. A long noodle fell off of his plate and fell onto his lap. He went to reach down to grab the noodle and his elbow bumped his plate and he got red spaghetti sauce all over his elbow and his plate fell down and shattered on the floor.

Listen Huey, we made you a good dinner and you let your plate fall onto the floor, but it was just an accident. I'm getting so tired of this, you always find a way to make a mess for your mom and I. Yes, I know, but it wasn't my fault. Of course it was your fault, honey stop blaming Huey, let's just eat and stop the blame game. Hey, yes honey, I knew that we shouldn't have used the fine china tonight.

Oh top worrying about the dishes, Huey didn't mean to do it and you still want to blame him for it. He probably feels bad about it and might have lost his appetite for dinner. You know those fine dishes came from my great grandmother who I didn't know a lot about. I didn't want those dishes to become broken.

I can't just go to the store and buy another set of these dishes. Listen honey you are being overly dramatic, now that's enough. Can't you just finish your dinner then complain later, I'm not very hungry and soon I want to excuse myself from the dinner table.

"Why don't you ask how Alexis if she's enjoying her dinner?"

"I will do that then"

"How's your dinner?"

It would be better if you didn't argue with my brother. I'm sorry for that, it's just lately I'm getting upset over everything and anything. Maybe you should go to the shrink.

"Where did you hear shrink from?"

"I heard you say that yesterday."

You shouldn't worry about adult things until you're older, I really care about you and I think you need some help. You're right but I'm stubborn and don't want to leave you kids alone. Just take some time and go get some help, honey I agree with our daughter.

You do need some help or you will get worse and we don't want to see you get worse. You have been struggling lately, we all can tell. Now you are making a mountain out of a mole hill over the dishes. You don't hear me complain about a broken dish, these dishes were my great grandmothers and ment so much to me.

"What if your dishes got broken?"

"I wouldn't mind"

I mean I don't understand what the big deal is, let's drop the subject honey and get on with dinner.

"Is everyone done eating?"

"Yes," Huey and I have finished up eating

"Now it's time for us to wash the dishes."

"Who wants to start the dishes first?"

I will mom, go ahead and then let your brother help you to dry the dishes. Your dad and I are going to go up to the bedroom for a short while and were going to talk. We won't be watching you kids wash the dishes, do a good job washing the dishes. Let's go, you and I need to talk.

"What are we going to talk about?"

"You will find out once we get upstairs to the bedroom."

I'm walking up the stairs a lot quicker than you are. Walk faster, honey I'm coming hold on.

"What's the matter honey?"

"I just feel like I'm out of breath."

Mr. Ruffalo finally got upstairs and flopped down on his King sized bed. You must be so tired, should I tuck you into bed, no, thanks. I will get up after five minutes. I'm all sweaty and I have a bad tooth ache.

"Are you still feeling out of breath?"

"No," not so much right now.

Listen honey, you have been losing your temper more often and I don't like it. You need to stop yelling at the kids. I know, I should have not let the broken dish make me that angry. I just lost my cool and I really didn't mean it, then I want you to apologize to your son when we get back down stairs. Don't just say yes to me honey, you must do it. Our son and daughter love us both very much.

"Do you promise me that you will not yell at the kids for the rest of the night?"

"Yes," I promise that I won't.

Why don't you take off that silly red cape. I can't believe you walked up the steps with that long red cape on. It wasn't so bad, you could have tripped and fell down.

If you don't want to take the cape off, then why don't you wrestle around on the floor with the kids. That sounds like a good idea honey, I might as well play with son then. You will have fun I know it.

> "Aren't you going to hug me?"

> "No," maybe later I will.

Oh honey you aren't as much fun as you used to be.

> "Would you stop it with that?"

> "No," honey, it's the truth

Why does it hurt when I talk about it. I don't know, I'm tired and grumpy, then why don't you take a nap and come down and play later then. That sounds good to me, just stay laying there on the bed honey and close your eyes. I will be back to check on you in an hour or so.

> "Is that okay honey?"

> "That's fine with me."

Mr. Ruffalo was feeling so relaxed that he was ready to go into a dream state. Lauren slowly walked down the steps and was watching the kids at the sink.

Stop splashing me with the cold water, or I'm going to tell mom. Please don't do that, I was just trying to have some fun with you.

> "Hey kids?"

> "Yes," mom, you two aren't behaving, why don't you stop splashing around in the water and finish the dishes.

> "What happened to dad?"

> "He's fine, he's just resting and will be out soon to play with you kids."

> "Did he fall or something?"

> "No," he didn't, he's fine.

I'm tired of him getting mad mom, I wish he would calm down and be nicer to my brother. He will be, I just got done talking to him. We're going to finish up the dishes now, now get your little hands in motion and finish cleaning the dishes.

Huey's already done drying the few dishes, mom I'm done washing the dishes. My arms are getting tired from scrubbing the dishes, I know sweetheart but you have to keep going. I get the same way sometimes, I want you to stand next to your brother and I want you to give him a hug and telling him that it's going to be okay. I can tell that he's frantically in need of a hug, I don't want a hug from my sister.

"Why not?"

"I'm not happy with her?"

She's always trying to get me into trouble with you mom, she's like a tattle tale and I'm tired of it mom. I will talk to your sister about it, listen kids I think that I'm going to have a shrink come here to the house tomorrow.

Don't tell your dad about it, want him to be surprised and happy that I looked for help for him. Your dad's a good man it's just he isn't in a good place right now in his mind.

I can see that he's eating more to keep himself happy, and I think he needs to try to go on a diet. I have done some research on diets and I want to try to get him to start with one of the well-known dicts. Wow you have a lot to say today.

"What do you kids think about dad going on a diet?"

"We think that it would be a good idea, and want what's best for our dad"

"What's the name of the shrink mom?"

"His name is Mr. Brighten."

"How long has he been a shrink for mom?"

"All of his life."

A friend of the family gave me his number and I called him while you kids were playing and while your dad was outside walking. I want you kids to be on your best behavior when he comes over, he's doing me a great favor by coming to the house. He doesn't usually come to his patient's house, but he's only doing it for me and no one else.

"Is he an old man?"

"No," he's a year or two older then dad.

"Does he know who Elmo and Big Bird are?"

"Yes," he knows who they are.

Mom I had a dream that Elmo came over in a dream I had last night, that was a silly dream.

"Do you like Elmo that much?"

"Yes," I do mom.

"How about you?"

"I don't like Elmo or big bird, I like the big blue Cookie Monster."

I like how he's always eating cookies, you know that dad used to eat too many cookies in his younger years. I didn't know that mom, yes it's true. Kids why don't you go sit in the living room and watch Barney or see what else is on television.

No, thank you, we would rather run around in the backyard, what's up with you two wanting to play in the backyard, it's a large space where we can run around freely. We like the fresh air, and besides that it smells like burnt bread in here and stinks like a clove of garlic.

"Mom can we please tag with each other?"

"Yes, you can just be careful and don't trip and get hurt."

Huey and Alexis went running to the back door and slung open the door and just continued on running. You forgot to close the back door, we're so sorry mom. Their son walked over to the door and gently pulled it shut.

Let's go play hide and seek, and hopefully then dad will come out and play with us. Meanwhile there dad's, one front tooth was really hurting and he couldn't bare the pain of it. So he stood up and walked over into the bathroom and looked in the mirror.

He switched the light on and began to star at himself in the mirror, his hair was a mess and looked like a bird's nest. Some long hairs were hanging out all over the place. His eyes looked like they were getting glassed over and he let out a big yawn, and pulled his mouth open with his hand and looked at his discolored teeth.

All of his teeth were yellow and he pushed his right pointer finger against the sore tooth, then for some odd reason smelled his finger, and smelled like it was rotting away. It was so stinky that it caused him to back up against the bathroom door. He stopped looking in the mirror at himself, and turned the bathroom light off.

He walked up to his bedroom door and slowly opened it and began to walk down the steps. He was still wearing the red cape, once at the bottom of the steps Lauren looked up at him from the couch.

"Hey honey, what's going on?"

"Not much I just have a bad tooth ache."

"Which tooth is it?"

"It's my front tooth."

Honey you have awful breath.

"Why don't you do rinse your mouth out with some mouth rinse?"

"I'm going too"

The kids are already out in the backyard playing hide and seek.

"Why don't you go join them?"

"I think I will."

After you rinse your mouth out, If you didn't have such a big heart honey I would have divorced you a long time ago. I love how you have a big kind heart, thanks honey I love you too.

"What made you bring up the topic of divorce anyway?"

"I was reading an article in this health magazine about it."

I don't like that word divorce, it's make my heart beat much faster and thus it's not good for me.

"How's your heart beating right now honey?"

"Have we talked about our wills yet?"

"Yes," and we have plenty of time to make them up with the nice friendly lawyer.

I don't think lawyers are that friendly. They just like to take your hard earned money away, but honey they also help you. If you say so my love, I can find my own legal advice on the internet on my own good time.

As he was walking away from his wife he kept on mumbling and was complaining. Hey honey, I can hear you complaining all the way over there. Just let me go, things will be better that way.

He walked up the steps again and walked into his bathroom and opened the bottle of mouth wash, he leaned his head back and gargled the mouth wash around in his mouth. He turned the water on and leaned over and spit the mouth wash into the sink.

The mouth wash made his gums burn, and he shook his head and walked out of the bathroom. He walked down the steps and walked out into the living room. Lauren was still sitting on the couch reading her magazine, she looked up from the magazine and peered across the room.

"Hey honey, how are you doing now?"

"I'm doing good"

I just got done rinsing my mouth out and I'm tired of it making my gums burn, Maybe you have a gum disease. No, I don't.

"Why would you say that?"

"That's what it sounds like to me."

You're no dentist, so don't guess.

"Why did you just say an insult like that to me honey?"

"I'm not feeling good and I'm not in the mood to talk."

"What's it going to take to make you happy honey?"

"I don't know and I don't care."

What an attitude you have this evening, I get tired of you putting me down, I didn't mean it though, that's not true.

"Must you always put the last word in?"

"Yes," I do and this why were close to breaking up.

I will be taking the kids and you won't have them, that's not right and you know it. So stop talking like that I mean it, you're talking so cruel right now.

"Are you really going to get a divorce?"

"No," but it's just a warning to you.

I think on that note, I will go spend the rest of the evening with my kids. Mr. Ruffalo looked back at his wife and she gave him a dirty look. I hope you have fun with the kid's honey, you gave me such a dirty look. Just forget about what we were talking about honey.

"I'm not going to forget it"

"How about that?"

"Stop it honey."

"What are you looking at?"

"I'm looking at our kids playing so nicely together."

Were so blessed to have two good kids, the kids aren't always well behaved though honey. They're kids and aren't perfect.

"Are you perfect?"

"No," I'm not, and I make mistakes too.

That's what I thought, you're being such a critic with everything. No, I'm not honey.

"What's your problem honey?"

"I don't have a problem."

I think that we should spend some time alone or were going to keep fighting. Why don't you go hang out with your friends. I think I'm going to wait here for the traveling dentist. She looked out the front window and saw a man coming, your dentist friend is here.

She opened the door and let him in, I presume your my patient Sir, yes I am. The man placed his briefcase down on the chair in the living room and began going through his dentistry tools. I'd appreciate it if you took a seat, now let me take a look.

After looking around in his mouth for several minutes, he found that one of his teeth were rotten, and one of your filings is coming out. The soonest appointment I can make for you is in two weeks, today's visit will be two-hundred and fifty dollars. He took out his wallet and gave the man the exact amount of cash, the man closed up his brief case and walked out.

"What did you think of that man?"

"I didn't like him, he had no personality"

"Are you going to call him back?"

"No"

I think he charged far too much, and he didn't take his time looking you over. He didn't even say a single word to me, but acted like I wasn't even there. He could've at least greeted me with a hello, but ignored me. He had the look of disgust on his face, I'm glad that he didn't use the tools on me, they probably weren't clean.

"Do you think he's a quack?"

"Yes I do."

Suddenly his wife left the room. Are you there? There was no answer, he raised his voice and yelled for his wife again and still no answer. He angrily said out loud forget you then, he slowly went walking outside and his son stopped what he was doing and looked up at his dad and so did his sister.

"What's the matter dad?"

"I'm feeling down and lost."

Were here for you, I know that kids but when you're an adult you have more problems then you're a kid.

"What kinds of problems?"

"I don't want to go into it."

"Why not?"

"I don't want to talk about"

"What have you kids been doing?"

"We have been playing with sticks."

That doesn't sound like any fun to me, we enjoy to play with the sticks and run around the backyard.

"How many times did you play hide and seek?"

"We played it three times then we got bored and began to play with the sticks."

He happened to look up into the tree in the backyard and saw that there was a large hornets nest on one of the branches of the tree. I want you both to get out of the backyard and get inside.

"Why?"

"There's a large hornets nest in the tree and I don't want you kids to get stung."

It's almost dark outside and the bees are probably sleeping, that's the best time to get them.

"Why must you kill them?"

"Because they aren't your friend and never will be."

If people can change so can the bees. No, bees don't change for anybody. No, matter if you talk to them or not, they will still sting you.

"Where's mom?"

"She went shopping and will be back soon."

"When will she be back ?"

"I honestly don't know?"

You're going 'to make me rip my hair out, too many questions? I'm just a very curious kid. I think instead of taking care of the bees you should go lay down again. No, I don't want to lay down, why don't you and your brother continue to run around the living room while I kill the bees.

We will let you to it then, there dad walked out by the tree and observed where the bees were flying in and out of the nest. He walked around to the front of the house and saw that his wife's car was no longer there. He saw that there was a lemonade stand, he thought to himself I sure could drink a cold glass of lemonade, but ignored the urge.

He walked over to the front of the garage and swung up the garage door and stepped into the garage. The garage had a musty odor to it and there was one window in the garage and there were cob webs all over it. He went over to the one shelf and began to look for a can of bee spray. He couldn't find a can of bee spray, he didn't stop looking.

He looked around in a cardboard box, and all he could find in there was an old mop and some cleaning products. To his astonishment on the bottom of the box was a small can of bee spray. He thought to himself I finally found some bee spray, he put the cardboard box back on the shelf and closed the garage door behind him.

He ran around the side of the house and observed the bees nest from a safe distance. He was hoping to see some bees flying around the outside of the nest. He remained there watching the bees nest but nothing was happening, this left him disappointed. He quickly ran over to the nest and sprayed the nest.

He ran backwards and tripped over a tree branch, but he still had his eyes focused on the bee's nest. Several bees fell out of the nest, and onto the ground. He thought to himself I got them good this time, later that night he watched some television with the kids and put the kids to sleep at eight fifty-five pm.

He walked into his bedroom and sat on the corner of the bed and thought to himself I feel like I'm losing control of this relationship with my wife. He thought things can't be that bad can they? He couldn't stop thinking about what his wife kept on saying to him. He laid back in his bed and still had negative thoughts in his mind.

After an hour of thinking so hard he drifted off to sleep and didn't care if he woke up or not. He forgot to turn the air conditioner on his bedroom and was sweating while he was sleeping.

Meanwhile his wife was shopping and she kept on thinking about their relationship. She sat down on a bench right outside of the clothing shop, and watching all the people walking past her. A couple that must of just been in their early twenties went walking by and a tear ran down her cheek.

The both of them realized that they were no longer a good match for each other. That night Lauren never returned home and Mr. Ruffalo kept on sleeping until ten the next morning, Lauren went and stayed at a hotel for the next week.

About the Author,

I'm 28 years old and was born with a debilitating condition known as Duchenne Muscular Dystrophy, a muscle wasting disease. Not long ago I spent 58 nights in a row fighting for my life with pneumonia. After I got home I discovered I was given a gift from God in the form of writing Angels, who talk to me and download stories into my mind that I then make books from. I've published over fifty books thus far, and plan to write more just as long as God will let me which I hope will be a very long time.